OLLIE and the TRAINERS

First published in Great Britain 1997 by Heinemann and Mammoth,
imprints of Reed International Books Ltd
Michelin House, 81 Fulham Rd, London, SW3 6RB
and Auckland and Melbourne

10 9 8 7 6 5 4 3 2 1

Text copyright © Rachel Anderson 1997
Illustrations copyright © Ken Cox 1997

The author has asserted her moral rights
The illustrator has asserted his moral rights

Paperback ISBN 0 7497 3109 5
Hardback ISBN 0 434 97939 2
A CIP catalogue record for this title is available
from the British Library

Printed and bound in China

Rachel Anderson

OLLIE and the TRAINERS

Illustrated by KEN COX

🍌 YELLOW BANANAS

For Nyamoi Fall Taylor

How Ollie Had No Trainers

ONCE UPON A time, not so long ago, there was a boy called Oliver Fork. Ollie was a contented sort of chap except for two things.

Thing One: Ollie had no trainers.

Thing Two: Ollie couldn't read words.

'Can't read yet?' laughed Alicia Dribble. 'Can't be bothered more like. Even the babies in Infants can read.'

But first, the trainers.

Some mornings, Ollie felt that he was the only person in the whole world who didn't have a decent pair.

In the playground there were Apaches and Gladiators, Ice and Thunder Zaps. There were Desert Snakes and Shadows. There were Wombats, Hercules, and Night Tigers.

Ollie knew the names by heart even though he couldn't read them.

Ollie's own shoes had no names on them. He wore a pair of old black lace-ups with thin soles, worn-down heels and splitting sides.

Ollie lurked in a corner of the playground so that nobody would see them.

But Alicia Dribble came by. She saw.

'Tee hee hee! Look at Ollie Fork!' she crowed. 'What stupid shoes! Like a pair of rotten boats!'

Alicia had a new pair of Desert Snakes. She was a show-off. They had cost her mum a proper packet.

'Nobody wears old clompers like that any more!' she laughed.

'Shove off, you,' said Ollie.

Lee Ling came over. 'Don't take any notice of her,' he said. Lee Ling was Ollie's friend. He never laughed at Ollie.

At that moment the whistle went. It was time to go in.

How Lee Ling Had
A Good Idea

AFTER SCHOOL, LEE had an idea.

'Let's go home past the new sportswear shop,' he said. 'We can look at the trainers.'

The shop was full of signs, on the door, on the walls, on the shelves. Ollie asked Lee what they said.

'Oh, nothing important,' said Lee.

But it was important to Ollie.

'Wow!' said Lee. 'Look! There are trainers for cross-training. Aerobics. Circuit training. Racket sports. Brill!'

Ollie looked. When he was younger, not being able to read didn't matter. But it mattered now. He wanted to read about the trainers for himself.

'These have got torque!' said Lee. 'With intersole springform. They're all High Performance.'

'High prices too,' said Ollie. Ollie wasn't much good at words. But he was good at reading money. His dad had shown him. His dad said if you hadn't got much, then you darn well had to be good at counting it.

'They've got all the best styles here,' said Lee. 'I'm going to ask my mum to get some of these for Chinese New Year.'

Ollie wished he could ask his dad to get him things he needed, at Chinese New Year, or ordinary New Year, or Christmas. Or anytime.

Before Ollie reached home it began to rain. It came in through the splits in the bottom of the black lace-ups. First, it made Ollie's socks wet, then his feet.

'Saw some great trainers in the new sportswear shop, Dad,' said Ollie. 'Called Gladiators. They've got full intersole springform and torque.'

But times were tough
for Ollie and his dad.

'Sorry, son,' said Dad. 'We can't stretch to
trainers this week. Another time, maybe.'

In the morning, Dad got a long piece of
sticky tape and fixed it round Ollie's shoe
so that he could go to school.

How the Reading Lady
Had an Idea

ON WEDNESDAYS, OLLIE went to his special session with the Reading Lady while the rest of his class did Painting.

'Tee hee hee,' laughed Alicia Dribble. 'Who can't read yet? Who misses out on Painting?' Alicia could read so well she had a Good Reading Badge.

'I hate Painting. I like going to the Reading Lady,' Ollie said.

'But even the babies in Infants know how to read!'

'Don't take any notice,' said Lee.

So Ollie pretended not to mind. But inside he did.

Ollie liked the Reading Lady. She was kind. She had lots of books full of pictures and not too many words. When he got fed up with trying to read the words, the Reading Lady read to him instead.

After listening to her reading for a while, Ollie told her his troubles.

'Well now, fancy that!' said the Reading Lady. 'It just so happens, I know the very place where your father could get you some new trainers. At a fair price too.'

'Proper trainers?' asked Ollie.

'Very proper.'

On Thursday it rained some more. On Friday, the sole came off Ollie's other shoe. On Saturday, Mr Fork took him to the footwear shop.

It was at the other side of town by the railway. The shoes in the window looked a bit dusty. There were no high performance trainers.

'It's no good, Dad. Come on, let's go,' said Ollie.

'No harm in asking, is there?' said Mr Fork.

The bell over the door jangled as they went in. There was no footwear on display inside. Instead, cardboard boxes were stacked from floor to ceiling.

'Dad,' Ollie whispered. 'It's spooky. I don't like it.'

But it was too
late to leave.
'Aha!' said the
shopkeeper, as
though he'd been
waiting for them
to turn up.
'Here we are then.'
He climbed slowly up his
stepladder and then took
down a shoe box from
the top of the pile.
He handed it to Ollie's dad.
'These'll be the ones for him,' he
said.Ollie heard a strange noise.

It was like a hen clucking as it laid an egg. It seemed to come from inside the box.

'They're not a well-known brand,' the shopkeeper said, 'but they have all the usual high quality features. Plus a few extras. I believe you will find they are the boy's size exactly.'

Ollie wondered how he knew when he hadn't even bothered to measure his feet.

'That'll be one pound please, sir,' said the shopkeeper.

'A pound?' said Mr Fork. 'That's very reasonable.'

'They've been reduced specially for you. And if the young man decides he doesn't like them, you may return them. Bring them back in their original box, within ninety days, and I will refund double-your-money.'

Ollie's dad was very pleased.

The shopkeeper tied string around the shoe box, and knotted it tightly.

'That'll keep them in,' he said.

Ollie wondered what he meant.

How Ollie Got to Meet
His Trainers

BACK HOME, OLLIE took the trainers out of
their box to check them over. He could guess
why they'd been reduced. They were a weird
colour, not at all like proper trainers.

But at least they had
air-cushioned soles,
double tongue,
velcro straps,
pump action,
fat chunky laces,
torque bar insert,

cushioned support ankle-band,
support insole.

Ollie tried them on. The shopkeeper had
guessed precisely right. They fitted so well
it was like wearing a pair of soft slippers.

But just as he was going to show Dad,
someone said, 'Ha, ha, ha! You wanted us
to be smart like Alicia Dribble's new Desert
Snakes, didn't you?'

Another voice said, 'Well we're not. So
there. We're far smarter.'

Ollie looked down at his feet. It was the
trainers speaking!

'You wanted Wombats or Gladiators, didn't
you?' said one of them.

'You didn't think you wanted us, did you?'
said the other. 'Well, we're not any of that
common lot, are we, Paul?'

'No, we are not. We're Secret Readers.
And if you don't believe us, look underneath.'

'On our soles.'

Ollie sat down, turned his foot over and
looked at the sole of the trainer. There was

Secret Readers in tiny writing all over it, plus in the centre,

"FITS ANY SIZE."

Ollie wondered what it said. He wished Lee

was there to read it for him.

'Go on then. Read it!'

'Don't want to,' Ollie said.

'D'you hear that, Paul? Says he doesn't want to. What a dimwit.'

'Who's Paul?' Ollie said.

'Me,' said the left-foot trainer. 'And he's Peter. Don't go getting us muddled up. We hate that.'

'I thought you said you were called Secret Readers?'

'That's just a surname.'

'I never knew shoes had surnames.'

'Then it's high time you did.'

'You've got a lot to learn.'

'But if you treat us right, we'd like to help

you with your homework.'

'Don't need help. Don't do homework.'

'Don't do homework? Of course you do.
Everyone does homework.'

Ollie heard his dad calling him for his tea.
Ollie pulled both trainers off, pushed them
roughly back into their box, shoved the box
under the bed and went down to tea in
his socks.

'Dad,' said Ollie. 'You know those trainers you got me?'

'Yes, son? One sausage or two?'

'Dad, they talk.'

'Do they?' said Dad. 'That's great.'

'No, it isn't. I don't like the things they say.'

But Ollie could tell his dad wasn't really listening. He was too busy cooking.

How the Trainers Went to School with Ollie

WHETHER HE LIKED them or not, Ollie had to wear the Secret Readers to school. They started chattering as soon as he set off down the road. They were very bossy.

'Look where you're going,' ordered Leftfoot Paul.

'Yes, watch your step,' said Rightfoot Peter. 'There are a lot of words about. You nearly stood on that one on the manhole cover.'

'If you aren't careful, you might read one of them by mistake.'

'Then you'd find you were reading.'

They went on nagging Ollie all the way to school.

Everybody at school noticed Ollie's trainers.

'They're really brill,' said Lee.

'Show us, Ollie.'

'What kind are they?'

'They're called Secret Readers,' said Ollie.

Alicia Dribble sauntered over to see what was going on. 'Oh yeah? Secret Readers?' she sneered. 'Well I've never heard of them. Weird kind of colour. Sort of sicky. Bet he got them from the cut-price shop down by the railway.'

Ollie decided not to mention that they could speak, not even to Lee. He didn't want it getting around.

Luckily, the trainers kept quiet all day until, halfway home, they suddenly started on him.

'Hey you, up there! Mister Bean Head. You listening?'

Ollie looked own. It was Leftfoot Paul.

'Yes you, Oliver Fork! We've been observing you all day long.'

'And the reason you're not learning is because you waste too much time day-dreaming.'

'So you've got to concentrate more, specially about where you put your feet.'

'Don't keep telling me what to do all the time. It gets on my nerves.'

'Why d'you think we're called trainers? Because that's what we do. We train you!'

'Now, watch where you are going!'

Ollie looked down just in time to avoid
walking the trainers through a muddy puddle.

Glancing downwards, he noticed not only
the muddy water on the pavement, but also
some letters.

GAS

Ollie said the letters out loud. They made
a word.

'Gas!' he said.

'Yes?' said Rightfoot Peter. 'So what about it?'

'It's just here!' said Ollie. 'A word. On the pavement. It says "Gas".'

'Of course it says "Gas". That's because there's a gas main underneath the manhole cover.'

'But I read it!' said Ollie.

'Of course you did.'

'Try another.'

Ollie looked down.

He found:

Water

'It says "Water".'

'It does. It also says

FIRE HYDRANT

S p r i n k l e r

STOP VALVE INSIDE

Ollie was so surprised that he'd got 'water' right he didn't mind about the other words. 'I read it myself!' he said.

All the way home, there were other words waiting to be read. The trainers pointed them out to him. There was:

POLICE

No Waiting

Post Office

LADIES   **GENTS**

TELEPHONE

BEWARE of the dog

N O   W A I T I N G   A T   A N Y   T I M E

Ollie could read them all, almost without help.

'Easy peasy, isn't it?' said Leftfoot Paul.

'Once you get the feel of it,' said Rightfoot Peter.

And Ollie agreed. But when he went to see the Reading Lady on Wednesday, it wasn't so easy after all.

How the Trainers
Had a Snooze

THE READING LADY was always pleased to
see Ollie. And she always found time to chat.

'So you managed to get those special
trainers?' she said. 'Oh my, I am glad. They
look very smart.'

'They can talk,' Ollie told her. 'They've been
helping me. They're called Secret Readers.'

The Reading Lady didn't seem surprised.
'Splendid,' she said and chose a story which
she'd already read to Ollie several times. But
Ollie didn't recognise a single word. And the
trainers wouldn't help. Were they pretending
to be asleep?

'Perhaps your Secret Readers are feeling a
bit shy today?' said the Reading Lady. 'Never
mind. I'll read to you instead.'

'No!' said Ollie, folding his arms crossly.

'Well, perhaps you'd like to take this book
home with you?' said the Reading Lady.

'No,' said Ollie. 'I won't!'

He was in a mood with the trainers. It was all their fault, not helping him like they had before.

'You told me you were going to help,' Ollie said afterwards. 'But you didn't. You made me look really stupid in front of the Reading Lady.'

They wouldn't answer Ollie directly. Instead they began talking to each other about him.

'Lazy and uncooperative, that's what he is,' said Leftfoot Paul.

'Yes, but at least he can read "Gas" all by himself,' said Rightfoot Peter.

'That's not going to be much use to me when I'm grown-up,' snapped Ollie. 'Just being able to read "Gas".'

'What about "Water"? Water's very useful stuff.'

'You made me look silly,' wailed Ollie. 'You made me think I could read.'

'He should have borrowed that interesting book the Reading Lady offered him.'

How Ollie Realised
He Could Read

SO, THE NEXT day, Ollie asked his class
teacher if he could borrow a book from the
Reading Corner to take home with him.

'Well done,' hissed Leftfoot Paul. 'At least
that's a start.'

At home, while Dad was getting tea, Ollie
sat on the floor and stared at the cover. He
couldn't even read the title.

'It's too difficult,' he whined.

'Why not have a guess,' said Rightfoot Peter. 'What's the picture on the front?'

'Some pirates on a ship,' said Ollie.

'Good,' said Leftfoot Paul. 'So what d'you think it might be about?'

'Pirates, of course,' said Ollie crossly. 'And a ship.'

'And if you wrote a book about some pirates and their ship what would you call it?'

Ollie thought. 'I'd call it *The Pirates' Ship.*'

'Bravo!'

'Well done!'

The Secret Readers both cheered so loudly Ollie thought the neighbours would hear through the wall.

'Now try opening the book,' said Leftfoot Paul. Ollie opened it.

There was a picture of a pirate who looked a bit like Ollie's dad.

Rightfoot Peter said, 'What does it say?'

Leftfoot Paul gave him a clue. 'How do most stories begin?'

'Once upon a time?' Ollie suggested.

He was right. That was just how *The Pirates' Ship* began.

The Secret Readers cheered again.

Ollie felt a tiny bit pleased with himself. So he tried some more.

'Once upon a time,' he read, 'there was a pirate called Jim.'

Once he had read the first ten words, it seemed a waste to stop so he carried on to page two, then page three. By the time tea was ready, Ollie had read the book right to the end, which was page eight.

That may not have been many pages for someone like Alicia Dribble, but it was a lot for Ollie.

'So now you've read a whole book right through,' said Leftfoot Paul.

'With only a very little bit of help,' said Rightfoot Peter.

After tea, Ollie read the book to his dad, with a little bit of help. Then he found he could read his dad's shopping list without any help at all. That was because he knew the sort of things that his dad usually bought, so he could guess.

Beans
Milk
Tea
Bread
Apples
Veg

What Ollie Did Next

'SO YOU SEE,' said Leftfoot Paul, 'you could read all along. And now you've realised it, there'll be no stopping you.'

Ollie's dad took him down to the recreation ground to kick a ball about until it was bedtime. Ollie could see words everywhere he looked, all just asking to be read.

And even the ones he wasn't sure about,
like 'Royal Mail Collection Times', he was able
to guess at and still get right.
'Oh! Oh! Oh!' he shouted. 'I can, yes I can!'
At first his dad thought he was getting excited

about kicking the ball. When Ollie read out
the whole list of Bye-Laws and Regulations at
the entrance to the recreation ground, his dad
suddenly realised and gave him a huge hug.

The next time Ollie went to the Reading

Lady, he read three whole books to her. She only had to help him with a few of the extra long words like, Llanfairpwllgwyngyllgogery-chwyrndrobwllllantysiliogogogoch and floccinaucinihilipilification.

Lee was impressed. But Alicia Dribble was annoyed. She got hold of Ollie in the playground and shook him.

'You're trying to catch up with me, aren't you?' she said. 'You just want to get a Good Reading badge like me.'

Ollie smiled and nodded.

Alicia scowled. 'I'll find out your clever tricks, don't you worry,' she said.

The next Saturday morning something very odd and rather upsetting began to happen. Ollie got dressed as usual. But when he tried to put on the trainers, they wouldn't fit.

He pulled. He tugged. He spoke to them. He pleaded with them. He undid the laces right down to the end. But he still couldn't get his feet into them. He wondered if his feet had got bigger or the trainers had shrunk.

His feet felt much the same as usual.

'It's you who've changed, isn't it?' he said to the trainers.

But they never said another word, at least not to Ollie.

'Well, I never,' said Ollie's dad. 'I know you've been growing fast, son, but this is quite something!'

So, after breakfast, Ollie put on his dad's big wellies and they walked back to the cut-price footwear shop near the railway.

The shopkeeper was standing in the
doorway looking down the street, almost as
though he was expecting them.

'No good then?' he said, beaming.

'Oh yes,' said Ollie. 'Very good. Very high
performance.'

'Except that they don't fit now,' said Mr
Fork. 'He can't get them on.'

'Then I will have to return your money, and
double it, as I promised.'

'That's all very well,' said Mr Fork, 'but my
son still needs something to wear on his feet.'

'Perhaps then,' suggested the shopkeeper, 'I should select another pair of trainers instead?'

As he put the Secret Readers' box back up on the top shelf, Ollie thought he heard some self-satisfied clucking coming from under the lid. But he couldn't be sure.

The new trainers didn't look much like anyone else's in the playground. And they couldn't speak. But they fitted! And they gave Ollie an extra spring in his step. Even Alicia Dribble noticed.

When Ollie walked up to collect his Good Reading Badge, he felt he was a mile high.

Have you enjoyed this Yellow Banana? There are plenty more to read. Why not try one of these exciting new stories:

A Funny sort of Dog *by Elizabeth Laird*
There's something not quite right about Simon's new puppy, Tip. It's very big with long claws, and it climbs trees. Then one day it roars and Simon has to face the truth . . . perhaps Tip isn't a dog at all!

Ghostly Guests *by Penelope Lively*
When the Brown family move to a new house, Marion and Simon discover there are three ghosts already living there! The ghosts make their lives unbearable – how can the children get rid of them?

Carole's Camel
Carole is left a rather unusual present – a camel called Umberto. It's great to ride him to school and everyone loves him, even if he is rather smelly. But looking after a real camel can cause a lot of problems. Perhaps she should find him a more suitable home . . .

The Pony that went to Sea *by K.M. Peyton*
Paddy, an old forgotten pony is adopted by Tom and Emily Tarboy. One stormy night, Paddy is taken aboard the houseboat where the children live. But during the night the boat breaks free from its moorings and is carried out to sea. It's up to Paddy to save the day.

Bella's Den *by Berlie Doherty*
Moving to the country, my only friend is Bella. One day she shows me her secret – a den. We go there one night and see some foxes, and in my excitement I blurt out what I've seen and a farmer overhears. He says foxes kill lambs and later he sets off to hunt them down. I've got to stop him . . .